THIS LITTLE TIGER BOOK BELONGS TO:

_____

_____

_____

_____

*For Simon, Julie*
*and the new baby*
~L.C.

*For Sue*
~G.R.

LITTLE TIGER PRESS
An imprint of Magi Publications
1 The Coda Centre, 189 Munster Road, London SW6 6AW
This paperback edition published 1999
First published in Great Britain 1999
Text © 1999 Linda Cornwell
Illustrations © 1999 Gavin Rowe
Linda Cornwell and Gavin Rowe have asserted their rights
to be identified as the author and illustrator of this work
under the Copyright, Designs and Patents Act, 1988.
Printed in Belgium by Proost NV, Turnhout
All rights reserved
ISBN 1 85430 602 2
3 5 7 9 10 8 6 4 2

# BABY SEAL
# ALL ALONE

*by* Linda Cornwell

*illustrated by* Gavin Rowe

LITTLE TIGER PRESS

*London*

When Baby Seal was born, the sun shone round and golden in the sky. "Baby Seal has been born!" called the gulls overhead and they flew down to admire the seal pup's white coat.

Soon Father Seal took Baby Seal to the edge of the rocks and she slid gently into the water. She glided like silk as the great waves washed over her.

Each day Baby Seal played all alone
in the water.
Each day she looked out over the
vast sea with her big eyes.
And each day she learned more
about her bright, wide world.

One day a great eagle
swooped down with loudly
beating wings.
SWISH! SWISH! SWISH!
he went.

The eagle snatched up a
shiny silver fish right out of the sea.
"How exciting and clever he is," said
Baby Seal. She wanted to play with the big bird.
But her mother warned her to take care.
"The eagle is so **BIG** and you are so small,"
she said.
Before Baby Seal could play with him, the eagle
flew away into the blue sky.

Baby Seal played every day all alone in the water.
One day a huge whale swam by. She spouted
water from the blowhole on the top of her head.
It sprayed high, high, HIGH into the air. The whale
smacked her huge tail on the waves.

SMACK! SPLASH! SMACK!

"How exciting and clever she is!" said Baby Seal.
She wanted to play with the whale.
But her mother warned her to take care. "The whale
is so BIG and you are so small," she said.
And before Baby Seal had time to play,
the whale swam far, far away.

Baby Seal played every day
all alone in the water.
One day a big white snowball
came rolling down the hill –
down, down, faster and faster.
It grew bigger and bigger!

**WHOOOOOOSH!**
went the snowball, bumping
and tumbling along until . . .

BUMP – it broke to pieces on the edge of the sea.
Out from the snowball struggled a big, white
polar bear!
"How exciting and clever he is!" cried Baby Seal.
She wanted to play with the funny, white bear.
But her mother warned her to take care.
"The bear is so BIG," she said.
"And you are so small."
Before Baby Seal could play
with him, the bear had
bounded off up the hill.

One day a reindeer came trotting by. He sang
*very* loudly. *"WHOOOO, WHOOOOO!"*
What a noise! But Baby Seal liked his song.
"How exciting and clever he is!" she said
and she began to sing her own song.
*"YIP, MYIP, MYIP, YIP, MYIP, MYIP!"*
She wanted to sing and play with the reindeer all
day long. But her mother warned her to take care.
"The reindeer is so BIG and you are so small,"
she said. And before Baby Seal could play with
him, the reindeer ran away across the rocks.

The days passed and Baby Seal played
every day, all alone, in the water.

She dived . . .

and she splashed . . .

and she swam.

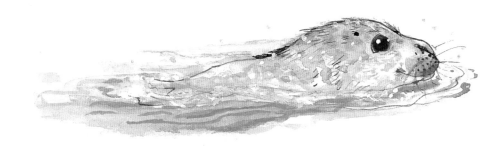

As time went by, Baby Seal grew and
her white coat changed to a mottled grey.

One night, as Baby Seal
snuggled close to her mother
and father, gazing up at
the twinkly stars with her
big eyes, she said to herself,
"I wish I was clever
and exciting and quite,
quite grown up and I wish
I didn't have to play all alone."
The next day there was a
BIG surprise . . .

Another baby seal had been born!
The eagle
and the whale
and the bear
and the reindeer
ALL came along to take a peep.

"You must take care of the
new seal," Father Seal told her.
"Because you are so BIG and
she is so small!"
And Baby Seal couldn't help
thinking that her little sister was the
most exciting and clever thing of all.

Join the LITTLE TIGER CLUB now for lots more books to enjoy!

Schools can join too and will receive a special enrolment pack.

Little Tiger's big surprise!
Julie Sykes · Tim Warnes

Laura's Star
Klaus Baumgart

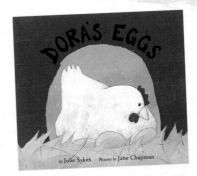
DORA'S EGGS
by Julie Sykes    Pictures by Jane Chapman

Mouse, Look Out!
Judy Waite
Illustrated by Norma Burgin

JOIN THE LITTLE TIGER CLUB

Once you've become a member of the Little Tiger Club, you will receive details of special offers, competitions and news of new books. Why not write a book review? The best reviews received will be published on book covers or in the Little Tiger Press catalogue.

MARK EZRA
The Prickly Hedgehog
Pictures by GAVIN ROWE

Smudge
Julie Sykes and Jane Chapman

The LITTLE TIGER CLUB is free to join. Members can cancel their membership at any time, and are under no obligation to purchase any books. If you would like details of the Little Tiger Club or a catalogue of books please contact:
Little Tiger Press, 1 The Coda Centre, 189 Munster Road London SW6 6AW, UK. Telephone: 020 7385 6333
**Visit our website at: www.littletiger.okukbooks.com**